Only Children Hear Me

Only Children Hear Me

Jake is a Friend You Can Talk To

A Novel

Mary L. Byrne

iUniverse, Inc.

New York Lincoln Shanghai

Only Children Hear Me
Jake is a Friend You Can Talk To

iUniverse books may be ordered through booksellers or by contacting:

iUniverse
2021 Pine Lake Road, Suite 100
Lincoln, NE 68512
www.iuniverse.com
1-800-Authors (1-800-288-4677)

Because of the dynamic nature of the Internet, any Web addresses or links contained in this book may have changed since publication and may no longer be valid.

This is a work of fiction. All of the characters, names, incidents, organizations, and dialogue in this novel are either the products of the author's imagination or are used fictitiously.

ISBN: 978-0-595-44359-8 (pbk)
ISBN: 978-0-595-88688-3 (ebk)

Printed in the United States of America

Contents

Acknowledgements

I am so proud to have my story in this book to share with everyone. I received a lot of help from some really great people and I'd like to thank them.

First, there's my breeder Marianne Dwight of Fox Hill English Shepherds, Shelburne, Massachusetts. Thank you for my excellent breeding and for selling me to my people parents. You knew I wasn't cut out for the farm.

Bob Fontaine, my photographer, took several pictures of me in his Warwick, R.I. studio. He caught the great pose of me on the cover of this book. Thank you for your patience and kindness, it was greatly appreciated.

Mark Davis of MJA Media is my web site designer. He spent a lot of time designing my web site to allow me to communicate with all of my friends. Thank you for helping me to make my special dream a reality.

Susan Charbonneau of Chica Ink, Wickford, R.I. is the sweet lady that helped Mom to create my footprint rubber stamp for the last page of this book. Thank you for all your help.

Special thanks to my wonderful Veterinarian, Dr. Sharon Chang, of Big River Veterinary Services, West Greenwich, RI. You've always been so kind, patient and understanding with me and I appreciate it so very much. You're a very special lady.

To my family and friends that have encouraged me not to give up on my project, thank you from the bottom of my heart.

Chapter 1

The Farm

A farm was a wonderful place to be born, especially a dairy farm. My mother told us the story so many times, I remember all the details. She said it was one of the coldest February mornings she could remember. She and the other herders had just brought the cows in for their morning milking, when suddenly she had to leave. There wasn't time to tell anyone where she was going, she just ran to the tack room.

No one noticed Mom leave; they all wondered where she could be? Everyone looked for her. They couldn't find her in the barn and she wasn't out in the corral. She wanted to bark to let everyone know where she was but she was just too busy. She was giving birth to her puppies.

Jason finally found her in a box, in the corner of the tack room.

Jason was twelve; he was the oldest of the five Smith children. He helped with a lot of chores on the farm and had seen many puppies born, but he still thought it was such a beautiful sight. When he found Mom she had just delivered the second puppy. He sat beside her and watched as she delivered two more. Jason was always amazed at how newborn puppies would squirm as they were being cleaned by their mother. Our little eyes were still shut but we tried to find her nipples to drink. We were born hungry. Most of us were black, brown and white just like Mom, but a few of us were reddish brown and white like our Dad Oakie.

Jason knew he had to tell his mother that Maggie was having her puppies, so he forced himself to leave. He wondered how many there would be when he got back.

He ran up to the house yelling, "Mom, Maggie's having her puppies."

His mother came out of the kitchen and asked him, "What's all the yelling about?"

"Maggie's having her puppies right now," Jason told her.

They both ran back to the barn together. When they got there she already had five puppies, and was giving birth to the sixth one. They sat with Mom as she gave birth to the last two of us. She had a family of eight. There were six boys and two girls. We were too young to be picked up so Jason just sat and looked at us.

He said, "Mom, I think birth is amazing."

Jason's brothers and sisters came running out to the barn to see us. Jason didn't want the kids to handle us until we were bigger and able to get around by ourselves. He felt very protective of my Mom and her new family. He let them look at us for a minute then he said,

"Let's go kids, the puppies are too little for you to touch and it's time to get ready for school." Then he took the kids back to the house.

Jason came back to the barn to help his dad with the milking, before he got ready for school, as he did every morning. He yelled to his father, "Dad come quick, Maggie's had her puppies and you have to see them." His father didn't have time to stop so he yelled out to Jason, "I'll see them later, I have to milk these cows and get the feed out."

The farm was a very busy place. There was a lot of hard work to do everyday. Even the youngest of the Smith children had chores. Mom's job was to herd the cows when they were out in the pasture. Now that she'd had her puppies one of the other dogs would do her chores. When we were old enough to go to our new homes she'd go back to herding.

Jason's mother took pictures of us and mailed them to everyone on her waiting list.

She said, "I hope it makes it easier for everyone to pick out the puppy they want, by seeing the pictures, before they come to the farm."

Over the next few weeks we grew a lot.

I overheard Mrs. Smith talking to Lilly when she called to make their appointment.

She said, "Hi Lilly, I've been expecting you to call. Yes, you and Frank will have the first choice of the puppies. You can come and see them tomorrow if you'd like to. I know you're anxious to see them. So what are you planning to name him? Jake's a very nice name. Okay, I'll see you tomorrow at eleven o'clock."

Now I knew the puppy they had chosen would be named Jake, but I had no idea it was me.

When they arrived at the farm both Lilly and Frank were shocked.

Lilly said, "I can't believe how big they've gotten since you sent us the pictures. But they still have their puppy fuzz and their noses are rounded. When they get older won't they be more pointed?"

Mrs. Smith said, "Yes they will and they'll be steadier on their feet then too."

We were still a little wobbly so we'd run and fall. Frank saw me and said, "There's the puppy we picked out in the pictures." I was so surprised to hear him say I was the puppy they had chosen. He said, "Look Lilly, he's adorable. He's making strange noises; it sounds like he's talking." Frank picked me up and I licked his face. He told Lilly, "This is the one we want, this is Jake."

Lilly just laughed and said, "It didn't take much for him to win your heart, just a kiss and a smell of his puppy breath."

Mrs. Smith told them, "You'll have to wait until Jake is eight weeks old to take him home with you, so I'll see you in four weeks."

The other puppies were running around playing with each other but I was more interested in playing with the kids. Since Frank and Lilly couldn't take me home for four more weeks, Frank asked Mrs. Smith to have everyone call me Jake, so I'd get used to my new name. I thought it sounded like a big boy's name.

I spent most of my time with the kids. Everywhere they went I was there too. Mom scolded me. She tried to teach me to herd but I just wanted to be with the kids. When my brothers and sisters were out in the pasture with Mom, I'd run off to look for the kids.

Mom told me, "You'll have to find a family without cows because you wouldn't know what to do with them." I knew mom was disappointed but herder's love children too, so maybe I wasn't so different. I was proud to be an English Shepherd but I was more interested in being a friend to the kids.

Finally, I was eight weeks old and it was time to go to my new home. I wasn't sure I was ready to leave the farm, my mother, or my brothers and sisters.

Mom nuzzled me and said, "I love you Jake and I'm very proud of you. You're a good boy. You've always known what you wanted. I'm glad you're going to live with a family instead of being on a farm. I know you'll be happy there. You'll always be my special son. I know life will be different for you. You won't be living on a farm like the rest of the puppies; you're going to the suburbs."

I told Mom, "I love you too, and my brothers and sisters. I know I'll miss all of you but I have to be with children. I think there is something special I'm meant to do. Please try to understand."

Mom said, "I do understand and I hope you'll be happy being with children. Take good care of yourself."

Mom said, "Jake, before you go there's something I have to tell you, please sit down here with me, and listen very carefully. Last night I had an amazing dream. Max, the guardian dog came to talk to me about you. He said a Higher Power has chosen you to be a friend and guardian for children everywhere. You are a dog in every way. Now you have the ability to talk to children, and the instinct to know when and how to guide them to help keep them safe. You can not talk to adults. Only children will hear you speak, and only until they mature and no longer need your guidance. This is why I was never able to interest you in herding; you were born to help children. Max will be your spiritual guide. Don't be frightened; he's your friend. He said you are the only dog that's ever been chosen for such an important job. I am so proud of you."

I asked my mom, "When will I be able to talk to kids?"

She said, "You can talk to them right now." Wow, I was shocked! Imagine me being chosen by a Higher Power to help kids? I knew I really loved children but I never thought I would be able to really make a difference.

I told mom, "I feel sad to be leaving my family and the kids but I have to. My adventure is just beginning. Frank and Lilly seem really nice and I think I'll be happy living with them. The best part is they don't have any cows. I'll do my very best to always make you proud of me."

Mom said, "I'm sure I'll always be proud of you."

Frank and Lilly were so surprised when they saw me that day.

"Frank said, the collar we brought will just about fit around Jake's neck, he was so much smaller when we bought it. Jake, since we're leaving the farm you'll have to wear a collar and be on a leash. I'll get you a new collar as soon as we get home. This one just won't do, it's too small, and you're going to be a big boy."

All of the kids ran out to say goodbye before we left. They were petting and hugging me. It was really nice to know they'd miss me. I licked them all goodbye. There were tears in my eyes. I had gotten very attached to all of them, and I knew I'd miss them.

As I walked toward the car with Lilly and Frank I stopped, and looked back at my mother and my brothers and sisters. I may never see them again and thinking about it made me cry. I was still just a puppy and I knew I'd miss everyone. I was the first of us to leave the farm to go to his new home. The rest of the puppies would be leaving in the next few days. Then Mom would go back to herding the cows; she said that was her job.

Suddenly I stiffened my legs to hold back as Frank was coaxing me to get into the car. I was still watching Mom and my brothers and sisters walk back to the barn. Then I realized that I had to go so I jumped into the car.

Frank and Lilly brought a basket for me to sleep in on the way home, but it was too small. Frank put it on the floor next to his feet. Every time he put me in the basket, I climbed out and tried to get up onto his lap. Frank finally gave in and I curled up and slept on his lap. Lilly later said while she was driving she looked over at us and we were both sleeping. She wondered what it would be like having me in their lives. She and Frank did a lot of research before choosing an English Shepherd. They already knew I had a mind of my own.

Frank and I napped most of the way home. When we stopped for me to take a potty break, Frank put on my leash before he opened the door.

He told me, "Jake, I know you don't like this but you can't run loose here or you might get hit by a car."

I really didn't like it but I'd have to get used to it.

Chapter 2

No More Cows

When we pulled into the driveway Lilly tapped Frank to wake him. I stretched and looked at both of them.

Lilly said, "Hey, do you want to see your new home?"

I jumped up; I sure did want to see my new home. Frank took me for a potty break in the woods, and then led me up the stairs to the house.

Wow, this isn't bad; I hadn't seen one cow since we got there! Frank took me into the house and straight to the kitchen. When I saw the gates I knew what they were for. I guessed I would be living in the kitchen.

Frank said, "Jake until you're housebroken you'll have to stay in the kitchen."

After just a few weeks I was housebroken and had full run of the house. Frank and Lilly were amazed at how smart I was. I learned everything so fast. They bought me my own bed and put it in the bedroom, on the floor next to their bed.

Lilly told me, "Jake you don't have to sleep in the kitchen anymore your bed is here next to ours."

Frank taught me several tricks. I knew my right from my left. I could roll over, sit and crawl. I could find my toys when they hid them and I even knew my colors. They knew I wasn't an ordinary dog. I was really different. They thought I was special. Frank and Lilly would soon find out how different I was!

I continued making noises that sounded like I was talking. Actually I was talking but adults couldn't hear me. I always got the last word.

I finally got my first visit from Max, the guardian dog. He appeared to me in a dream. He said, "Jake your mother, Maggie, told you that you've been chosen by a Higher Power to help children.

You'll be able to talk to them and help guide them through their lives until they're grown. I'll help you and answer any questions you have."

I asked Max, "Why was I chosen for such an important job?"

He answered, "Because you are a special dog. You're very kind hearted, you love children and want to make a difference in their lives. You were the perfect choice. You see, you don't have to try to be good, you just naturally are. I'm here to help you make the right decisions when children come to you."

I asked Max, "Do you think some of the kids might be afraid of me because I can talk to them?"

He said, "Maybe some will, you'll just have to convince them you are there to help them and they're safe. Eventually most children will come to trust you. If you should need to talk to me or there's something you can't handle on your own, just think hard about me and I'll come to you in your next dream."

I woke up thinking how lucky I was to be part of such a special assignment.

It didn't take very long for me to feel that Lilly and Frank were really my people parents, my new Mom and Dad. I wished they could hear me call them that but they couldn't. I'd have to be happy just thinking it to myself.

One afternoon Lilly's daughter Lynn stopped by with her two children, Melinda and Joey. I decided it was time to tell the kids I could talk. We went out into the yard and sat on the ground. I said, "I have something to tell you." As soon as I started to talk Melinda cried and jumped up, she said, "You're a dog! You're not supposed to be talking to us."

I tried to calm her down and I said, "Don't be frightened. I've been chosen by a Higher Power to talk to kids to help them. I can't talk to adults, but I'll be able to talk to you until you're grown, then you'll no longer hear my words. If you ever have a problem I'll try to help you. If you just want to talk I'll be here."

Melinda stopped crying and finally smiled. She said, "I guess it's really great that we can talk to you. I'm sorry I got upset, but I've never heard a dog talk before."

I told her, "I understand how you feel. I hope you'll soon be comfortable with me talking to you. Maybe you could tell your friends about me, too."

She said she would and warned me that she would probably ask me all kinds of questions.

I saw my mom look out the window to check on the kids. She saw the three of us sitting on the ground. Melinda and Joey were nodding their heads and talking to me. Mom had a strange look on her face. She looked puzzled but decided that we were fine, and so she went back to her conversation with Lynn.

Melinda said their parents were divorced when they were both very young.

Melinda asked me, "Jake do you know how we can get our parents to go back together? We love them both and we really want to be a family again. What can we do to help them?"

I told them if their parents were ever going to get back together it would have to be because they wanted to, not just because their kids wanted it.

Then Joey said, "But everyone would be happy if we were all together, and Dad wouldn't be living by himself and be lonely."

I told them, "All you can do is love both of your parents, and enjoy the time you spend with each of them, when you're together. You can't fix everything by just wishing it away, it would be nice if it were that easy, but it isn't."

They understood even though I didn't give them the answers they really wanted.

Melinda thought about it and finally said, "Jake, I know you're right; we'll have to be patient and hope that some day things get better."

When Mom called the kids in for drinks and cookies I went in with them. Melinda ran in all out of breath. She said, "Nana we had a problem and discussed it with Jake, he gave us some really good advice. He's a real good friend to me and Joey. Jake really can talk but only children can hear him. I'm only telling you because he'll need you to drive him when he has to visit with kids that need his advice."

Mom told them, "Jake's smart and unusual and sometimes it actually sounds like he can talk, but honey, he's a dog." Melinda and Joey spoke at the same time and told her she was wrong.

They said, "Jake really can talk, but you can't hear him because you're a grown up."

Mom told me later she didn't believe what the kids were telling her but she said, "Yeah, okay." She thought both of her grandchildren had a great imagination. She knew the kids both loved me and figured it would pass. Lynn came back to pick up the kids and Mom said she tried to put the whole thing out of her mind.

Early the next morning I was running off the deck and I caught my right foot between the boards. Suddenly I felt severe pain shoot through my whole leg and I couldn't walk. I was so scared. I didn't know what was going to happen to me. Mom rushed me to my Veterinarian, Doctor Chang.

She examined my knee and she said, "Jake has torn the inside of his knee. We'll try some medication for a couple of weeks but if he doesn't get better, Jake will have to have surgery. Sometimes the pills help to heal the tear. We won't know that until we've tried the medication."

Mom took me home and gave me the first pill. It was awful. She had to put it way down in the back of my mouth, then make me swallow it by rubbing my throat. I gagged and fought not to spit it out. I wanted to get better so I finally swallowed it and got a drink as fast as I could. For the longest time I could still taste that bitter pill taste. No matter what I ate it was still there.

For two long weeks I took those horrible pills. I hobbled around. My knee hurt, and I wasn't able to step on my foot. It didn't get any better no matter how many pills I took. I went back to the doctor for my follow-up check-up. Doctor Chang said there wasn't any improvement, so she called the surgeon, Doctor Clark.

Doctor Clark agreed to see me that night so Mom and Dad brought me back at seven o'clock. I hobbled in on three legs for my appointment. He examined my knee and moved it back and forth. Wow, that really hurt.

He said, "I'm afraid no amount of medication will fix Jake's knee. We'll have to operate to repair the tear. He'll have to be restricted for ten weeks so he won't reinjure his knee."

Dad asked him, "Doctor, when will you operate on Jake?"

Doctor Clark said he could schedule it for the following Monday, which was only three days away. Everyone agreed and we headed back home.

I had to be very calm for the next three days. That wasn't hard because I couldn't walk on my foot and I was having a lot of pain. I tried to imagine how I'd feel after the surgery, so I could be prepared for what was going to happen. Finally, I decided I'd have to wait to see how I'd feel when the surgery was over. If I ever wanted to get better and walk and run again I had to have the operation, but I was really scared.

Mom and Dad brought me to the hospital on Monday morning. They petted me and gave me a hug before the nurse took me into the back room. She put me onto a big metal table and raised it into the air so she could reach my leg.

Doctor Clark came in and shaved my front leg then put a needle into it. I heard him say, "This will be over before you know it." Then I fell asleep.

When I woke up after my surgery I was a little confused. I wasn't sure at first where I was and what had happened. Then I began to remember why I was there. I looked down at my leg and saw that it was all shaved. I had a tube in my front leg connected to a bottle of what I guessed was medicine. I figured the surgery was over, so I wondered how long I'd have to stay in the hospital. I was still very sleepy and my leg hurt a lot. I must have fallen asleep again.

When I woke up the doctor was checking my leg and saying, "Well Jake you'll be much better now, we got you all fixed up." I was glad to hear that. Now I just wanted to go home to my very own bed.

The next morning Mom and Dad came to get me, so I had to get up. That sounded pretty simple until I tried to do it. I was still a bit foggy from the medicine they gave me, to put me to sleep. I was weak and in pain. I couldn't stand on my leg, so I had to try to balance myself on three legs, without falling down. It was really tough to do, but with everyone's help I finally made it. Before they let me go home they put this strange looking collar on me, so I wouldn't try to touch my stitches.

I was a mess! Two legs were shaved, I couldn't walk straight and I had on a collar. I hoped that nobody I knew would see me. It was very difficult for me to get into the car without hurting myself, so Dad helped me. The ride home was awful and I couldn't get comfortable. I felt like everything was hurting and I just wanted to go to sleep and wake up when I was all better.

During my recovery several of the kids from the neighborhood stopped by to see me.

Mom told them, "You'll have to be careful not to let Jake run or jump. He could hurt his knee even more."

The kids were good with me and always quiet. Mom told me later that she finally realized they always seemed to be talking, and listening to me. Some of the kids said things as they were leaving that sounded like the end of a conversation.

When Cindy, the little blonde haired girl from down the street, was leaving Mom asked her, "How was your visit? What did you and Jake talk about?"

Cindy told her Jake was just telling jokes.

Mom said, "I know you're just kidding with me. I have to finish cooking." Then she turned around and went back to the kitchen. She began to wonder if her grandchildren were really telling her the truth. Could I really talk? No, it was just too impossible to believe.

Mom tried talking to me herself. I couldn't say anything to her. I wanted to, but I could only talk to children.

I just made my usual noises. Mom pleaded with me, "Please Jake, talk to me."

I felt bad but I just couldn't talk to her, finally out of frustration she talked to Dad. I heard her tell him everything that had happened and what she was beginning to suspect.

Dad laughed. He just looked at Mom and said, "Lilly you can't actually expect me to believe that Jake talks to children, can you?"

Mom said, "I don't know what I expect you to believe. I'm not sure what I believe." Before she went to sleep I heard her say a special prayer. She asked that she be allowed to hear what was really true.

Mom told me she woke up the next morning chuckling. Imagine, she actually thought I might be able to talk to children. She felt better and went to the kitchen for breakfast. She was glad she didn't have to listen to Dad laugh at her again.

Mom walked into the kitchen and said, "Good morning Jake."

I responded by saying, "Good morning Mom."

Mom didn't know what to do. Had she just imagined that I said good morning? She quickly sat down at the table, looked at me and very calmly said, "What's going on?"

Chapter 3

Lilly Hears

I said, "Melinda and Joey told you the truth. I can talk, but only children hear me. You can hear me now only because you asked to hear what was really true. My dog mother, Maggie, told me about it before I left the farm. I was chosen by a Higher Power to guide children and help keep them safe. Max, the guardian dog, was sent by the Higher Power to be my spiritual guide. He explained it all to my mother in a dream. Max asked her to tell me before you brought me home. I'm the only dog that's ever had the ability to talk to children. I've been given this gift to guide children and help them whenever they need me."

Suddenly the phone rang and Mom said, "Hi Lynn, no I didn't see the book, but I'll look for it for you. I'll call you back in a little while and let you know if I found it."

Mom smiled and asked me to continue with what I was saying. So I said, "Please tell Dad that I can talk but he'll never be able to hear me. Children will hear my words until they become adults, then they will only hear noises like you did. Children with some disabilities will always hear me because they'll always be childlike. You've seen how many kids have already come to see me. Well, I've been able to give some of them advice about things that were bothering them. When some of the kids first found out I could talk, they were scared. It took time for me to explain to them how and why I'm able to talk to children"

Mom told me, "I'm very grateful that I can hear you. It's wonderful that you can talk to children. I'm just trying to get over the shock. Will I always be able to hear you?"

I told her now that she believed; she would always be able to hear me. Mom promised that she would talk to Dad as soon as he came home.

When he got there Mom told him everything. But Dad couldn't believe it. Hopefully in time he'd believe I had a gift, but he'd probably never hear me. I guess it's hard for some people to believe in something they can't really see and hear themselves.

As I continued to recover from my knee surgery I spent most of my time with Melinda, Joey and the neighborhood kids. Mom knew how much I enjoyed being with them. I was really happy when I could help them. Sometimes it was just a little discussion. Every now and then I was able to give them advice about something more serious.

We were out in the yard one afternoon when Lisa, the short girl with freckles, asked me, "Jake would you please explain to us what being "different races" means?"

I said, "Let me explain it this way, I'm tri-colored which means I'm black, brown and white. In the animal world being different colors is considered beautiful. Being a person of more than one race is beautiful too. Some people might be Caucasian and Asian or African American and Mexican"

George spoke up and said, "Hey, look at me, I'm Korean and American, and Patty is Mexican and Hawaiian. I guess we already know some kids that are more than one race, don't we?"

I knew they understood what I was saying so I told them, "We're all so different yet so special. Wouldn't it be boring if we were all the same? The color of our skin doesn't change our hearts or our souls; it just makes us look different from one another."

About a year later I hurt my left knee chasing the dog across the street. I had an operation to fix that one too. I decided it was time to really think about what I wanted to do when I got better. Sure, I could go back to being my old self. But I started to think about all the kids that might be hurting too. I've always loved helping children but I wanted to do more. I wanted to help as many kids as I could, but how was I going to reach everyone that might need my advice?

Mom spent a lot of time on her computer. I watched and she explained how it worked and all about web sites.

Suddenly I got a great idea.

I asked my mom, "Would you help me start my own web site on the Internet? Kids could send me messages and I could answer them, with your help?"

She said. "Yes, of course I'll help you, I think it's a great idea."

I asked Mom if she thought all kids had computers.

She said, "No, there probably are a lot of people that don't have them, they would have to write to you through the mail. I could rent a post office box for you then you could receive their mail, too."

Then all kids would be able to reach me either by e-mail or regular mail. Now I'd have to go out and meet a lot of kids, and give them my addresses. I hoped kids that needed my advice would ask for it.

Sally, Melinda's cousin, said, "That sounds great Jake, but what kinds of things do you think kids might want to talk to you about?"

I told her, "Some kids may have hurt their knees and had stitches; others may have broken an arm climbing a tree. Others might have a different kind of hurt that hurts on the inside, where most people can't see it. I want to help kids with whatever might be hurting them. When my knee gets better, I'm going to start helping kids everywhere and that will make me a very happy dog."

Sally asked me, "Can we write to you too, if we have a question or a problem?" I told her, "Of course, you can write to me anytime you need to."

When I woke up the next morning Mom told me, "It's been eleven days since your operation so the doctor is taking your stitches out today. Dad will take you to the Veterinarian right after breakfast."

I was scared and excited, all at once. Right after breakfast Dad said, "Let's go Jake, we're going to see Doctor Chang."

Dad lifted me up onto the front seat of his truck. I loved to ride in the front seat next to Dad; he petted me all the time we were riding. I looked out of the window as we drove along. Oh boy, that building looked familiar; it looked like the place where we'd gotten munchkins. I wondered if Dad was going to stop. Yes, he was, he was pulling into the parking lot. I must be in for a treat before we go to the doctors. It was hard to wait. I hadn't had a munchkin in a while and they were so good. I hoped Dad wouldn't forget I liked the plain ones. I couldn't go in with him; I had to wait in the truck. Most people thought I was just a dog and health rules said you couldn't take animals into places that served food, unless it was a Seeing Eye Dog.

Dad finally came out with the munchkins. I imagined I could smell them before he got to the truck. I thought, "Hurry Dad, you don't want them to get stale."

Finally Dad gave me my plain munchkins. I ate them very slowly. I only got two and I wanted them to last as long as possible. They were so good; I wished I could have them every day. If I ate them more often I'd probably look like a cow dog instead of a herder, and it wouldn't be healthy for me.

When we finished our treats, it was time to go to the Veterinarian.

It only took a few minutes before Dad was pulling into the parking lot. I was getting nervous and we hadn't even gotten out of the truck! Maybe I could just keep my stitches. No, I had to be brave. How could I help my friends to be brave if I wasn't?

As we walked inside I could see all of the other nervous dogs and cats. Wow, even the big Rottweiler was shaking; I didn't think they were afraid of anything. I guess none of us wanted to be there.

We weren't waiting long when I heard them call my name, "Jake, it's your turn." When we got inside the examining room Dad lifted me up onto the big metal examining table. Doctor Chang was already there. She pushed the button to make the table go up higher so she could reach my knee to take out my stitches.

She said, "Just relax Jake I'll try not to hurt you."

I hoped they wouldn't let me fall, it was getting really high, and I was really shaking.

Dad told me, "Its okay Jake; this won't hurt."

The doctor was very gentle. In just a few minutes she'd removed all of my stitches. Boy, I was glad that was over.

Doctor Chang told Dad, "Jake can't run or jump for another eight weeks. He'll need another check up in two weeks to be sure he's healing right."

Gosh, I thought I'd be able to start helping kids right away, now I'd have to wait until I was better! I had a funny feeling when my knee was healed I wouldn't be able to run like I could before I got hurt. I thought I might be slower than I was before I hurt my knees. I'd have to make some adjustments in my life.

When we got home I asked Mom if she thought I'd be totally like my old self when I was healed.

She said, "Sometimes things happen to us and it makes us different from the way we were before, and different from other people. Maybe you'll be even better. Some kids can't do all the things that other kids can. Maybe they can't run, just like you. Maybe they can't even walk. They're just as special as the kids that can walk and run. There are things they can do just as well, maybe even better than other people can. If you take the time to get to know them, you'll probably see what's special about them." I told her, "Thanks Mom, I understand what you're try-ing to tell me. Maybe I won't be just like my old self, but maybe I'll be better in some ways."

Mom just smiled.

Two weeks after my operation, I was putting my bad leg on the floor, just a little bit. It still hurt but it was beginning to feel better. Boy, it was hard to get around on just three legs. It took me longer to get everywhere. Mom and Dad had to take me out on my leash so I wouldn't walk too fast or run. I could do more damage to my knee. They knew if I was loose I might get the urge to chase a rabbit. I might forget I wasn't supposed to run. I just couldn't help it; I loved to chase rabbits. So far, I had never caught any, but it was so much fun to chase them.

I had to stay in the kitchen because I got so excited when company came. I always ran to the front door and jumped up at the window to see who was there. I just loved company. It was nice when someone new came to visit because I got so much attention. I got to act cute when Dad had me do my tricks. Then I got extra biscuits. For a real special treat, Dad put peanut butter on them. I loved biscuits, but biscuits with peanut butter on them were almost as good as munchkins. My parents spoiled me.

My family has a mother, a father, and me, Jake. My people parents adopted me when I was a little puppy. They really wanted a dog and I really needed a family. It was getting crowded on the farm where I was born. A lot of us are adopted and make new families, just like I did with my Mom and Dad. You don't have to be born into a family; you just have to want to be a family. You can come to need each other, take care of one another, and finally love each other.

Some families have a mother, a father and children. Some have a mother and children, or a father and children. Others have a grandmother and children, or foster parents and children. There's no right or wrong way to be a family. It's really about love and caring. You don't have to be relatives.

I'd be healed in eight more weeks then I could start talking to kids and making new friends, and maybe helping them with their problems. I was really excited. Some kids didn't have anyone to talk to about the things that really mattered. Sometimes they didn't have anyone they felt they could trust, with their really important problems or secrets. But they could trust me with anything they wanted to share. I'd give them my very best advice and help them stay safe.

Mom and I talked about what should go on the web site.

I told Mom, "I want it to be very easy for all my friends to get to my web site and e-mail me."

Mom suggested putting some pictures of me when I was a puppy and others as I was growing up, on the web site. We decided to call it "The

Photo Gallery." Next we had to find a web site designer to design it and make it work.

Luckily Mom had heard about Mark Davis, a web site designer that was located near by. She called him and he agreed to design it for us. I was lucky to have such an understanding and helpful Mom. Time was going by so fast. It wouldn't be long before I was able to get e-mails and mail from my friends.

After breakfast Mom told me, "We're having company for supper. Aunt Barbara, Uncle Pete and their kids, Jimmy and Susie are coming. I know you always love seeing them." I heard the car in front of the house. I was getting really excited. I had to keep telling myself not to jump or run or I could hurt my knee. I was going to have fun. I hadn't seen them in a while. Maybe the kids had gotten tall or I didn't grow, and they did. I felt short when kids began to get taller and left me behind.

At dinner Jimmy was very quiet. Even Susie couldn't get him to say very much, and she always got him talking. He just pushed the food around on his plate. He didn't eat much. I wondered what was bothering him. After supper I'd try to find a good time to talk to him. Maybe he'd tell me. I was worried to see him so troubled.

The adults were all talking, it was my chance to find out what was bothering Jimmy. We went into the family room.

I asked him, "Jimmy, do you feel like sharing what has made you so quiet tonight?"

Jimmy put his head down and didn't answer me. I waited a minute then I asked him again.

He finally said, "I got into trouble for coming home late from school and losing my back pack. Dad grounded me for three days. I lied to him. I told him I was late because I lost my backpack and I was trying to find it. Actually, an older boy in the neighborhood stole it from me. He threatened to beat me up if I told anyone what really happened. I was so scared; I told my father I lost it instead of telling him the truth. He said I was irresponsible. He grounded me to give me time to think about being more careful with my things. I felt terrible, I had never lied to my dad before and I didn't know what to do."

I thought Jimmy should tell his father the truth. The boy shouldn't be allowed to steal and threaten other kids in the neighborhood, he should be punished.

I knew Jimmy had to talk to his father so I told him, "I think you need to tell your father the truth and you should do it right away."

Jimmy agreed then he said, "I'm afraid Dad will be ashamed of me for being so scared."

I told him, "Give your dad a chance."

Jimmy went into the dining room and asked his father to come into the family room, so they could talk. Jimmy said, "Dad, I'm very sorry, I didn't tell you the truth about what happened to my back pack. I didn't lose it someone stole it from me. I was so ashamed I told you I lost it. I thought you'd be disappointed in me, because I couldn't defend myself against that boy."

Jimmy's father gave him a hug and said, "I'm sorry I punished you and accused you of being irresponsible. I should have tried harder to get you to tell me what really happened. Can you forgive me?" Jimmy smiled and said, "Of course I forgive you."

His dad said, "I don't ever want you to be afraid to tell me the truth about anything again." Jimmy promised he wouldn't. His dad told him he'd have to call the principal in the morning, and tell him the whole story.

Jimmy said, "I understand, I'm so sorry I didn't tell you right away. I'll never do anything like this again."

When it was time for them to leave Jimmy said to me, "Thank you so much for helping me talk to my dad. I feel so much better now that he knows the truth."

I was happy everything turned out so well. I'd had a very busy day but I didn't even have to climb the stairs to go to bed. That morning, Mom bought me a new bed and put it downstairs. She really spoiled me, and I loved it.

Chapter 4

Friend Donna

The next morning I was hanging around relaxing. I was still tired from the night before. Suddenly I heard my friend Holly, the Golden Retriever from next door, barking at the back door. Mom let her in, thank goodness, I thought she would wake the whole neighborhood.

I asked Holly in dog language, "What's all the barking about?" Holly was all out of breath. As soon as she calmed down a little she answered, "Jake, I had to come and tell you right away, I just couldn't wait until later. Our friend Donna, the girl from the playground, is very sick. Her mother told my mother that Donna has leukemia."

I said, "I'm sorry she's so sick. I'll have to go see her right away; maybe I can help. I'll ask my mom to take me. I still can't go loose until my knee is healed." I thanked Holly for coming to tell me. If she hadn't I wouldn't have known until my knee got better, and I was able to visit Donna on my own.

When I told Mom about Donna she understood why I needed to see her. I always like to visit with my sick friends. She called Donna's mother to be sure she was able to have company, before she took me to her house.

Donna's mom said, "She does have leukemia and she has started treatment. It makes her very tired, but she would be able to have a short visit with Jake. You'll both have to wear masks over your mouths so you don't give Donna any of your germs. She could get even sicker because she's weak from the chemotherapy."

Mom told her she understood and we'd be happy to wear masks to be able to visit Donna. I was really worried. I asked Mom if Donna would get better. Mom explained that leukemia treatment can take a long time, but she has a good chance of being better in the future. She explained to me exactly what it was and told me doctors and laboratories are working very hard to cure people with diseases like leukemia.

When we got to Donna's house, Donna's mom helped me put on a mask before I went to Donna's bedroom to see her. Mom stayed in the kitchen and talked with her mother. Donna looked so pale lying there on her bed. She opened her eyes when she heard me. I know she was happy to see me; she smiled when I walked in.

She asked, "How did you find out I was sick?"

I told her Holly had come to tell me.

Donna said, "I haven't had much company. Not many of the kids from school have even called me. I don't feel too good but I get really lonely. I miss all of my friends. Do you think my friends are afraid they'll catch what I have? Could that be why they are staying away and not calling?"

I wasn't sure how to answer her question so I thought about it for a minute. "I guess it's possible that some people don't really understand diseases like leukemia. They might think they can catch it. They may not know what to say to you. They may be afraid they would be bothering you when you need to rest."

Donna said, "I understand what you're saying but I really want to see and hear from my friends. They could wear masks when they come to visit, or they could call me on the phone. If I get too tired I could ask them to come back or call back another time." Her voice was pleading with me for help.

I asked Donna, "Would you like me to talk to your friends? I could tell them you'd like to see them or talk to them." She said she would like that very much.

Donna looked tired so I said, "I'm going to leave now but I'll be back soon." Donna was already closing her eyes as I walked out of her room.

As soon as we got into the car I told Mom, "I need to go to Donna's school to talk to her friends before we go home. Donna is really lonely and her friends haven't been visiting or calling her."

Mom said, "I understand, we'll go there right away." Mom stopped at the office to tell the principal we were there and get directions to Donna's class. The principal knew who I was because so many of the kids had talked to him about me. Mom walked me down to the classroom and waved to the teacher to come out into the hall. While Mom talked to the teacher about Donna, I went into the classroom to talk to the kids.

I said, "Hi, I'm Donna's friend Jake. I went to see her today. She misses all of you very much. She'd like to see anyone that wants to visit, or talk to anyone that wants to call her. If you'd like to visit, please call her mother first to make sure she's feeling well enough to have company. I guess you all know Donna has leukemia? Do you all know what leukemia is?" One boy raised his hand and said he didn't know. I explained, "It is a disease of her blood. It is making Donna very weak and tired. Her doctors are giving her medicine to make her better, but it will take a long time to treat. I'm not sure how long she'll be out of school. You can't catch what Donna has. It's very safe for you to visit her as long as you're not sick but if you even have a cold she could catch it from you. Donna could get much sicker because she is so weak." I told them they'd have to wear a mask to visit Donna.

I reminded them, "It's very lonely to be sick and away from your friends and your school. Donna can't get well by herself. She needs her doctor, her family and her friends." I thanked them for listening. The kids all thanked me for coming to tell them about Donna. I was pretty sure she would hear from her friends soon so I went home feeling better.

The next day it was already time for my four-week check up. Right after breakfast, Dad took me back to see my doctor. I still couldn't jump to get into the truck so Dad lifted me up onto the front seat. I couldn't wait until I could run and jump, and go for rides all the time. It was just a quick check up with no munchkins. I had to be careful what I ate. Munchkins were really good but if I ate too many I could gain weight, and that would be bad for my knee. I had to learn what was good for me to eat, even if it wasn't always what I wanted.

Before long we were pulling into the driveway at the doctor's office. Dad lifted me down from the front seat and we went in. I noticed that the collie and the poodle in the waiting room were shaking, they must have been nervous. Of course this time I wasn't scared myself. The doctor would check my knee and I'd be out of there. I couldn't seem to sit still and I wondered why. My legs were shaking. That was silly, I wasn't nervous so what was my problem? I guess I was just like all the other patients. Even if I was just there for a check up I was still frightened, like everyone else.

The receptionist called my name and Dad brought me into the examining room. He lifted me up onto the metal examining table. When Doctor Chang came in she took the time to talk to me and calm me down, before she started my check up.

She told me, "Everything will be fine," then she raised the table higher so she could check my knee. She moved it back and forth. It was still a little sore.

She said to Dad, "Jake seems to be healing just fine, but you have to be careful for six more weeks that he doesn't re-injure his knee. Then bring him back for his final check-up."

She turned to me and said, "Jake, you'll soon be back on all four feet."

Dad stopped at the desk to make my next appointment then we were on our way back home.

Boy, I loved to ride in the truck! I'd be so glad when I could do it all the time. It didn't take long to drive home. I saw two bunnies hopping across the grass as we drove down the driveway. I wished I could run. I'd chase after them but I'd never hurt them. I just loved to chase rabbits and try to catch them, but they were always too fast for me.

As soon as I went into the house Mom told me a boy named Bobby had come over to talk to me.

She said, "I told him you went to see the doctor. He went home to have lunch he'll be back about one o'clock. He's in Donna's class. He was at school yesterday when you spoke to the kids." Just as I was wondering why he wanted to talk to me, the doorbell rang.

Mom let him in and Bobby asked, "Jake, can I talk to you alone for a while?"

Of course I agreed. Mom left the room so we could talk.

Bobby said, "I have a problem I can't discuss with anyone else."

I was glad he felt he could trust me. I told Bobby he could talk to me about anything at all. Bobby said, "When I'm really hurt, I cry. My friends all call me a sissy. They say boys aren't supposed to cry. They tell me boys are supposed to be tough, and if I can't be tough, I should have been a girl. My father agrees with my friends, so he gets mad whenever I cry. He tells me to knock it off and grow up. I try really hard to be tough and not cry, but when something very sad happens, I do. I know my father is ashamed of me but I'm just a kid and I'm glad I can cry. I just wish everyone could understand how I feel. Do you think there's something wrong with me because I cry sometimes?"

I told him, "It's not wrong for boys to cry when something hurts them, it shows they have feelings. It really is okay for boys and men to cry. Some people think it means you're weak or there's something wrong with you, but that's not true. I think it's wonderful. You're a very special boy. Don't ever stop being sensitive. I hope some day more people will realize everyone has feelings and its okay to show them. I'm really glad you came to talk to me. Don't ever be afraid to talk to me about anything that bothers you."

Bobby promised me he'd come back then he left to go home.

Isn't it sad that so many people fight so hard to hide their feelings? They should spend more time being honest about what they feel.

Mom told me Donna called while I was talking to Bobby. She told Mom that her friends had started to call! A few of them even apologized for not visiting. They didn't think they could. A couple of the girls were going to her house that afternoon.

Donna sounded much happier. She asked Mom to thank me for going to her school. I was glad the kids had really listened to me.

I told Mom, "I think if you know someone who's sick you shouldn't forget them. If you can't visit for some reason you should call and let them know you're thinking about them. They'll feel so much better to know you care."

Since adults weren't able to hear me speak, the kids told their parents how much they liked visiting and playing with me, and about the great advice I gave them.

Some of their mothers stopped by our house to meet me. They told me they had never heard their children brag about a dog this way before. That made me very happy. Since the children had come to trust me, their parents didn't mind them visiting, as often as Mom allowed them to. Mom was making more cookies than usual but she didn't mind. I wanted to help as many kids as I could, and Mom did whatever she could to help me. I believe children are all special. They can be anything they want to be. I just want to help them stay safe.

The next few weeks went by fast. Mom was busy around the house and I had a lot of company. I thought a lot about Donna. I asked Mom to take me back to visit her and she agreed. She called her mother to see if she was well enough to have company.

Donna's mom said, "She's doing much better, you can definitely come over for a visit." I was so happy to hear the news I couldn't wait to see her.

I didn't have to wear a mask so I went right to her room. Our mothers stayed in the kitchen to give us time to talk. Donna was sitting at her desk doing homework when I walked in. It was great to see her out of bed. She looked so much better than the last time I saw her. She had more color in her face and she was smiling.

Donna said, "I'm really glad to see you. My friends all learned so much about my illness just listening to you. Now they all visit often. I have some great news. I'm finished with my treatments for now, so I'll be able to go back to school in a couple of weeks. I'm so excited to be going back."

I was so happy for her and glad I could help. We talked about my hopes of helping more children. So many of the neighborhood kids were stopping by to visit, and asking for my advice, it really made me happy.

I told Donna, "You have helped me, as much as I helped you. Just to see that beautiful smile on your face is all I need. You're my friend and I really care about you. Knowing you're going back to school is the best news." A couple of her friends stopped by so I promised to keep in touch with her, then I left.

While we were driving home I told Mom about Donna and how good it felt to help her.

I asked her, "Mom, are you sorry you didn't end up with a normal dog?" Mom told me, "I love having you in my life and doing my part to help you with the kids. I wouldn't change a thing."

She knew I had to share my gift with as many kids as I could. I just wasn't sure how to let them know I was there to help them. I couldn't just put an ad in the newspaper. I had to find a way to reach a lot of children. Otherwise it would take me forever, to let them know I was there to help them. I was sure I'd find a way with Mom's help.

Dad was at home when we got there. I really did enjoy spending time with him. It gave me a chance to be a regular dog. I just loved it when he scratched behind my ears and sat on the floor with me. My knee was getting better. I'd soon I'd be able to ride in the truck with him like old times.

That night I had another dream about Max. He asked me, "Are you having any problems that you need my help with?" I told him, "I'm doing fine so far. I'm grateful that I seem to know what to say and do when one of the kids needs my advice. There's nothing I can't handle right now, but I appreciate you asking."

Max told me, "Jake, you did a great job helping Donna. You made very good decisions with her friends at school. Please remember that I will always be able to help you if you should need me." I woke up smiling.

The very next day, one of the neighborhood mothers came over to talk to Mom. Mrs. Wilson, worked for a company that sponsored a summer camp for children with physical disabilities and behavioral problems. The children's doctors and counselors were sending them to a camp in Connecticut.

Mrs. Wilson said, "Jake's had such a positive effect on kids we'd like him to work as a mascot for the month of August. The camp is in the country about twenty miles from here. We'd love to have him there with us if you think he'd like to go?"

Mom couldn't answer without discussing it with me and Dad. She said, "I'll talk to Jake and my husband and let you know within the next two days." Mrs. Wilson said, "Thank you, we're hoping Jake will join us. I'll wait for your call."

I was so thrilled by the news I couldn't sit still! It was like a miracle! I couldn't imagine a better way to help a lot of kids at one time. Maybe I could make a real difference.

After Mrs. Wilson left, I told Mom, "I definitely want to go. By August my knee will be completely healed and I'll be ready for a trip to camp. I'll miss you and Dad and I know you'll miss me, but I'll be going to help the kids."

Mom agreed and said she'd explain to Dad why I wanted to go to camp, when he got home.

When Dad came home from work Mom told him about Mrs. Wilson's invitation.

Mom told Dad, "Jake has been chosen to be a mascot for kids at a special summer camp. It will be for the month of August, and he really wants to go."

Dad was upset that I'd be going away for a whole month but he realized it was important to me.

He finally said, "If Jake's being a mascot would make a real difference we have to let him go."

Mom called Mrs. Wilson to let her know I would be happy to attend their camp.

Chapter 5

Jake Goes To Camp

There were only two weeks left before camp and there was a lot to do. I had to tell all of my neighborhood friends where I was going and when I'd be back. I didn't want them to think I had deserted them. Friends have to consider each other's feelings. I would never deliberately hurt anyone. I always try to be thoughtful.

Peter, one of my neighborhood friends, asked me, "Why do you want to go to camp with troubled kids for a whole month?"

I gently reminded him, "I'm here to help all children, no matter what kind of problems they might have. Maybe these kids need my help a little bit more than most. Children with disabilities may have more limitations than you do. The kids with behavioral problems are probably no different than you are, except they may have had more painful experiences in their lives. Hopefully I can help a lot of them."

Peter apologized and said, "I'm sorry Jake, I didn't think about it that way. You definitely have to go and help kids that really need you. We'll all miss you but we'll see you when you get back. They picked the best dog to help those kids with their problems."

It made me feel good to know how they felt about me. I told everyone I'd see them as soon as I got back.

It wouldn't take me long to pack. I didn't have much stuff just my bones, my ball, two bowls and my new bed. I thought I'd be more comfortable if I had my favorite things with me.

I asked Mom, "Would you please get my stuff together for me?" Mom laughed and said, "Jake, you sound like a kid going to camp. Well, you are, you're our kid!"

How exciting it would be to work with kids from all over the country. This was the opportunity I had dreamed of. The idea of having children with disabilities and behavioral problems together was great. They could help each other, and hopefully, I could help them too.

Camp day finally arrived. I was tearing around the house making sure I hadn't forgotten anything. I was talking to myself as I went from one room to another. Dad had to leave early for work, so Mom said she would drive me to camp after breakfast. When Mom spoke to Mrs. Wilson she told her some of the kids and their counselors were driving to camp, but most were flying, or taking a train. They were coming from as far away as California. The program was planned by doctors and counselors from all over the country. A lot of the counselors would be going to camp to work with the kids themselves. All of the staff was trained to work with children with special needs. Being picked to work with them as a mascot was a real honor for me.

I was so quiet on our drive to camp Mom asked what was bothering me.

I told her, "I'm just a little nervous I'm being trusted to help all of those kids, I hope I'll do a good job. I'm also wondering if I'll get homesick.

I haven't been away from home since I left the farm. I really want to make a difference."

Mom said she knew I'd do my very best and that's all anyone could ask. She told me she and Dad would come up next Saturday if that was okay with me. I thought it was a great idea. I knew I'd really miss them.

The camp wasn't far and we got there in half an hour. Mrs. Wilson made it sound nice but I had no idea how large it was until we drove through the entrance. Enormous trees lined both sides of the driveway for as far as you could see. They seemed to bend toward each other, shading the driveway, yet allowing the sunshine to just twinkle through the leaves.

I could see little cabins through the trees. They all had screened-in porches with large numbers on the side of them. We drove past a lovely lake with a picnic area.

The camp was beautiful! I was excited just thinking of spending a whole month there.

I saw buses up ahead of us. They were parked outside of what looked like the main building. It had a big front porch, and was much larger than the cabins we saw on the way in.

Mom found a place to park and we went to look for Henry Jones, the Director.

We found him in the dining room. He smiled when he saw us.

He said, "We expect some confusion, but it should settle down pretty fast. Everyone's prepared to restore order quickly."

Mom told Mr. Jones, "The camp is beautiful. I hadn't expected anything quite like this."

He said, "I'll take you for a tour as soon as I finish checking the last of the supplies. Please feel free to look around the building."

Mom said, "I really want to see where you'll be spending the next month."

We wandered around. Mom said she was surprised at what she saw. She said, "The dining room is incredible, it's so big you almost can't count the tables."

Then we went into a game room, which was filled with so many fun things to do. Ping Pong tables and televisions with games filled one end of the room. At the other end there was a large screen television.

Mom said, "I don't know how big that television is but it's bigger than any I've seen at our local stores. They've thought of just about everything." We continued on to a craft room, where there were several long tables covered with craft supplies and paint and clay.

We were still in the craft room when Mr. Jones found us. He asked us, "Are you ready for that tour?"

Mom told him, "We certainly are."

We all walked from the main building past the neat rows of cabins down to the lake. There we found a lovely beach with beautiful soft white sand, and big colorful beach umbrellas. The lifeguard chairs that lined the water were so white they seemed to glow in the sunshine. A picnic area was in the middle of a large pine grove just beyond the beach. I could just picture the kids sitting at the wooden tables playing games.

Our next stop was the campfire area. There was a large stack of firewood ready for the first campfire. Large rocks were placed in a circle for seats around the fire.

Mr. Jones said, "We'll tell stories around the campfire and toast marshmallows by the bagful. This entire camp was designed for all the kids to enjoy. All the areas are handicap accessible and safe for everyone."

The cabins all had bunk beds. Mr. Jones explained that only the cabins for handicapped children had indoor plumbing. It was difficult to design an outhouse that special needs children could use. He said that some cabins had to be different depending on the children's needs. He pointed out that all the trails were carefully smoothed and leveled for a wheelchair to easily pass over.

Everyone could enjoy this beautiful camp.

We listened as Mr. Jones explained how it was designed and why. He said, "A great deal of time and work went into planning this wonderful place, for so many special kids."

When we finished our tour, Mom got ready to leave. She took my things out of her car and gave them to Mr. Jones. She seemed excited for me, but a little bit sad to be leaving me behind.

She told me, "We'll see you next Saturday."

I had butterflies in my stomach, but they were the good kind.

Mr. Jones told Mom, "I'm sure Jake will be fine! But I promise to call you if there are any problems."

She thanked him for the tour and said goodbye. We walked her to the car. Mom gave me a hug then got into the car. As she drove out past the buses I saw her smile.

Mr. Jones turned to me and said, "Let's go, Jake, we have a lot of work to do. Let's check the buses to be sure they're empty, then go to the main building and see how we can help." I felt really good about my camp assignment.

Mr. Jones told me, "The kids have been arriving all morning. While we were on our tour they began gathering in groups and went to their assigned cabins. They picked out their bunks and put their clothes away. Now they'll be going to the dining room for lunch. So we'll go there and see how it's going." I watched the counselors direct the kids to the right lines. Those in wheelchairs were served first. If they couldn't carry their trays on their laps some of the other kids helped them. Finally, everyone settled down and ate their lunch. I was sure I heard a sigh of relief from the counselors. Most of the kids were talking to each other as they ate, but some were very quiet. Hopefully they'd start talking as the days went on. We'd be at camp for a month, which should give everyone a chance to get to know each other.

After lunch we had to wait an hour to digest our food then everyone changed, got their towels, and headed for the lake. It was a perfect day to go swimming. I caught up with Mr. Jones for my instructions.

He told me, "Just watch how the kids are doing, and pay close attention to any problems you can help with." That's all I needed to hear! I was off and running after the kids.

When I got to the beach I walked around and spoke to them. Most of the kids seemed to accept me talking, but a couple of them backed off, and tried to get away from me. I went over to them and sat down.

I reassured them, "There's nothing to be afraid of, I won't hurt you. A Higher Power has given me the ability to talk to you. I'm here to help you with whatever problem you may have. I won't force you to talk to me. I hope you'll come to trust me, and realize I want to be your friend." I walked away hoping they really heard me and they'd eventually talk to me. Some of the kids actually said they thought it was great to be able to talk to a dog. I told them I'd be there to help if they needed me. Once everyone settled in I hoped they'd talk to me even more.

It was a beautiful August afternoon, and everyone wanted to go swimming. The water felt so warm and refreshing on my fur. I paddled around a bit then came out to lie in the sun and watch the kids. I decided to lie down beside a girl who was sitting all alone on her towel. She was just looking at the water and watching the other kids but didn't make any effort to join them.

I asked her, "Why aren't you going in the water?"

She told me, "I'm afraid of the water so I don't want to go in. I like to sit and watch the others have fun."

I thought something was wrong. I wanted to find out why she was afraid of the water. I told her, "Not everyone likes the water, some people just don't like to get wet."

She laughed and asked me, "How do they take a bath if they don't like to get wet?"

I told her, "Maybe they just don't like to swim in water that's over their heads. You can stand up in your bathtub. It's not over your head unless you're very short."

She laughed and told me I was silly. I knew I was making a new friend. I hoped she would talk to me. I asked her what her name was.

She told me, "I'm Brenda." I said, "Hi Brenda, I'm Jake, I'm sure glad to meet you." Then I asked her what she thought of the camp so far.

Brenda said, "I think it's beautiful." I told her, I thought we would have a lot of fun while we were there. Brenda said she thought so too.

I asked Brenda, "How about building a sand castle, I can dig and you build?"

Brenda said she didn't really feel like doing it today, maybe some other time. She seemed very sad. I had to find out what was bothering her.

I asked her, "Are you okay?"

She said she was.

I told her. "Brenda, I'm a good listener if you ever want to talk."

She said she would remember that. I thought Brenda wanted to be alone so I said I'd see her later.

As I walked back down the trail with the children heading towards the cabins, I saw a boy in a wheelchair. He had gone off the trail, and one of the wheels of his chair was stuck in the sand. He was so frustrated he was crying. No matter how hard he tried, he just couldn't get out. The kids continued on the trail and I went over and tried pushing against the wheel but it didn't help.

I told him, "Just relax, I'll go and get help."

I ran back to the office and found Mr. Jones sitting at his desk. I barked and reached up and pulled on his shirt with my teeth. Mr. Jones understood there was a problem. He followed me back to the boy in the wheelchair and pushed him out of the sand. I asked my new friend to thank Mr. Jones for me.

He said, "Thank you from me and Jake."

Mr. Jones said we were both welcome, and went back to his office.

I stayed with my new friend. I found out his name was Freddie, he was a good looking boy from Kentucky. We continued on the trail to the water. I wanted to be sure Freddie would be all right, before I left him. I asked him if he was looking forward to all of the camp activities.

He said, "I've always been in this chair. Most people think I can't do anything, so most of the time I don't try. I don't have many friends at home. The kids think it's boring to be with me, since I can't run and play with them. I get really lonely, but I don't know what to do about it."

I told him, "While you're here at camp you might find there are a lot of other kids here that have limitations too. When you go home you might want to ask your parents to check with your local WMCA. They may have sports programs for handicapped children. If they don't have a program they may be able to start one, especially if there's a need in your area. I think you'll be surprised how much fun you can have."

I asked Freddie, "What happened when you got stuck in the sand?"

Freddie said, "I was with some kids that had gone on ahead not realizing I was stuck. I thought I could get myself out, so I didn't yell to them. When I realized I couldn't, they were too far ahead to hear me."

I told Freddie I would be around so if he needed anything, he could just yell. We both laughed. Freddie thanked me again and went to the beach to join the other kids.

I continued walking toward the cabins to make sure none of the kids had stayed behind. Finding everything quiet, I walked back on the winding path toward the beach. I listened, and all I could hear were the birds and an occasional squirrel. It was so quiet I could hear my paw steps, and my breath, as I panted from the heat. What a beautiful and peaceful place this was. You could really feel and experience nature. Of course, I was a dog, so maybe I noticed it more than the kids would.

A lot of the kids were gathered in the picnic area to get out of the hot afternoon sun. Several large pine trees shaded the area, and all the tables had umbrellas. It was a nice place to go after a day of swimming. The counselors passed out checkers and other board games, to everyone sitting at the tables. The kids seemed comfortable in their new surroundings.

Chapter 6

Delightful Breakfast

We were spending so much time talking and playing ball, I had to rest whenever I got a chance. I missed chewing my bone and sleeping late, and I really needed a bath. I didn't want a bath because I hated them, but I loved the feeling of being and smelling clean. I would have to ask some of the kids to help me take one. I could go swimming myself but I couldn't put on my own shampoo.

I was talking to a couple of the boys I'd gotten to know pretty well so I said, "Would you mind giving me a bath down at the lake? I have my own shampoo, but I really need someone to rub it into my fur."

Jimmy and John, the twins from New York, said they'd do it. Since we had time, we decided to do it right away. We stopped to pick up my shampoo and went down to the lake.

Jimmy said, "Jake, why don't you just jump in and get wet then we'll put on the shampoo?"

It sounded good to me so I jumped in. The two of them poured on the shampoo and started rubbing it in. I had to admit it really felt good! When they finished I dove in to rinse off, then went back on the beach to dry.

I said, "I really appreciate my bath, guys, thanks again."

Boy I felt like a new dog, and I smelled like one too. With all the running around I did and my long fur, I really needed that bath.

When Mom and Dad arrived for their visit I was looking pretty good.

Mom noticed right away and she asked, "How did you take a bath?"

I told her, "I really needed one, so I asked a couple of the boys to help me. I feel so much better, and you know I don't like baths."

Mom smiled, she knew how much I hated them.

I told Mom, "It's great to have the kids talking to me more openly every day. Even the kids that were afraid of me at first are finally beginning to talk to me."

Mom and Dad stayed for dinner and went with me to story time, at the camp fire. Just before they left to go home Mom surprised me and said, "I have your new web site and post office box addresses I got them during the week. Now you can give them to the kids before they go home. They can keep in touch with you, and share your addresses with their friends, whenever they need you."

I asked her, "How did Mark get the web site up so fast?"

Mom said, "He was so interested in your project, he made it a top priority to finish it as quickly as he could. It looks great."

I said, "Thanks Mom, I really appreciate it." She just smiled. Mom was helping me in every way she could, and I was very grateful.

What a wonderful adventure this was. Maybe someday we could make a movie to help me reach children everywhere. I thought, wouldn't it be incredible to be as well known as Mickey Mouse? I could stand for peace and happiness, hope and safety for children. I had to be serious. I wasn't Mickey Mouse, but I wanted kids everywhere to know how very special they were, and that they all deserved the very best in life.

Anyone could achieve his or her hopes and dreams. They just had to want it badly enough to never give up, never stop trying. My job was to help keep all children from being mistreated.

After Mom and Dad left to go home, I went to check on the kids. Most of them were so tired they'd gone right to bed. The first week had gone by fast, I was glad we still had three more left.

It rained the next morning but I knew we'd have a fun day inside. There was so much to do, nobody would be bored. The cooks made homemade waffles with strawberries, peaches and whipped cream; and pancakes with fruit flavored syrups and powdered sugar. They also had cereal for anyone that didn't like waffles or pancakes. There were fresh baked muffins, bagels and toast with orange, cranberry or apple juice, and hot chocolate or milk. I wished I could sample everything, it all smelled so good.

Mr. Jones told the kids, "You can sit anywhere you want today, you don't have to stay with your own group. You might enjoy sitting with some of the other kids."

A very interesting thing happened! Most of them sat with kids they had never talked to before. It seemed like everyone just needed permission to find out what the other kids were really like. It was a great breakfast.

Afterwards Chris, a very tall boy from Texas, ran up to me and said, "I thought kids in wheel chairs were all geeks, but these kids are really pretty cool, they're not like I thought they were. I guess I'm learning."

I told him, "I think it's great that you're getting to meet so many different kids and maybe changing your opinion about them."

Chris smiled and ran off to join the others. The counselors planned games and crafts for the morning in the main building, so no one had to go out in the rain.

Mr. Jones told me that during the morning staff meeting the counselors decided to mix the groups for the rest of the day. They wanted all the kids to spend the day together, and help each other. After the day time activities every-one went back to their cabins to clean up, change for supper, and get some exercise.

Tommy, a very soft spoken boy, came over to talk to me. He said, "I always thought that being handicapped meant you had to be in a wheel-chair or something else like that. Now I see there are other ways to be handicapped."

I wanted Mr. Jones to know what Tommy said to me, so I asked him, "Would you be willing to repeat what you told me, to Mr. Jones?"

Tommy said, "Sure, I'll tell him if you want me to."

We walked to his office together. Mr. Jones waved us in when we got to his office.

When Tommy told Mr. Jones what he had said to me, Mr. Jones smiled, then looked at me and said, "Jake, it's working, keep it up."

I felt like skipping as we walked back to the dining room.

Tommy said, "We just got here and I'm already so happy I came, I know being here will help me a lot."

I told him, "I'm happy you're doing so well, remember I'll be here if you need me for anything."

Then I walked around the dining room and spoke to several of the other kids.

Everyone met with their counselor everyday, and had group meetings after supper. It was a very thorough program. Some of the kids told me they felt safe for the first time in their lives.

I told the kids when I first met them, "You can share anything with me, both good and bad. I'll never judge you and I will always listen. If I don't have the answer I'll send you to the right person to get the help you need." They could talk about little things or real serious problems. It was up to them.

During that night's meetings I decided to go for a walk and get some air. It had stopped raining and was very nice outside. As I crossed the porch I noticed Brenda sitting on the steps all alone. I hadn't talked to her since we first met on the beach. I wondered why she was out there all alone. She should have been attending one of the meetings. I walked over and sat down beside her. She looked so unhappy. I looked at her and asked, "Could you use someone to talk to?"

Brenda looked up at me with tears in her eyes. She said, "I wouldn't know where to begin."

I told her, "You could start anywhere you like; I'm not in a hurry."

For a while she just talked about home and school. She said she felt out of place since it happened. She wouldn't say what had happened. I just listened and let Brenda talk.

Finally, Brenda told me, "I wanted to talk to my counselors, because I wanted them to help me, but I was afraid."

I asked her what she was afraid of.

Brenda said, "I was afraid of what my uncle would do to me, if he found out I told anyone. He told me I was a really bad person, and that it was my fault."

I told Brenda, "You're not a bad person at all. I'm sure that what happened was not your fault."

Brenda started to cry. She said, "I really miss being a little girl and playing with my friends. My uncle watches me after school, because my mother works. He won't let me go out with my friends he makes me stay in with him and play."

I asked her what they played and Brenda just cried harder.

I felt so bad for her. The first time I met her I knew something was really hurting her. Brenda said, "My uncle has been touching me in my private parts, where he shouldn't be. I'm so ashamed. I was so scared all the time. I was afraid that my uncle would really hurt me, like he threatened to do. I didn't know what to do or how to make him stop. I was afraid to tell anyone, but I wanted someone else to know what was happening."

I told Brenda, "I'm so glad you've been able to tell me, now we can help you, and make sure your uncle never hurts you again."

She said, "My mother took me to a counselor at home. I was afraid to tell the truth because my uncle threatened me."

I told her, "You're safe now. You're with friends, and we won't let anyone hurt you again." I assured Brenda everything was going to be better now.

I asked her, "Would you be willing to talk to your counselor, if I go and get her?"

Brenda said she would.

I was sure her counselor could help with all the pain Brenda was feeling. I told her, "You are so special and no one has a right to ever hurt you."

I asked Brenda to please wait while I went to find Susan, her counselor. She promised me she wouldn't leave. I ran back into the building and searched for Susan.

Finally, I saw her on the other side of the dining room. I told myself to calm down. I didn't want everyone to realize there was a problem. I walked over to Susan and pulled on the leg of her jeans. She knew there was a problem and followed me back outside. I led her to the porch where Brenda was still sitting on the steps, crying.

Susan sat beside Brenda and held her, while she continued to cry. After a while she stopped crying and told Susan what she had discussed with me.

Susan told her, "I'm glad you were able to talk to me and Jake. We will help you. I promise you, your uncle will never be able to hurt you again."

Brenda was relieved after talking to us. She said, "I feel hopeful, for the first time in a long time. I know you and Susan are here with me, and I'll be safe. I really wish I could have met you a long time ago, but I'm glad I came to camp and found you now. Maybe someday, I'll feel like a little girl again."

I stayed with her for a long time. We talked about all kinds of things, until she was ready to go back to her cabin.

Brenda said, "I'll talk to Susan again tomorrow, thank you for being here for me, and for understanding."

I told her, "I'll always be there when ever you need me. If anyone ever touches you again in any way they shouldn't, please tell a grown up right away."

She said, "I will, thank you Jake, I'll see you in the morning."

The sun was shining when I woke up. I felt so good just knowing I was making a difference. I wouldn't rest until children everywhere knew all they had to do was reach out. I would help them in any way I could. I walked around the cabins to check on everyone. What an exciting time it was, the kids were just starting to wake up and head for the showers. Early morning was always noisy. But it was nice to hear the kids laughing, as they got ready for breakfast. The calm environment seemed to be good for everyone.

Both of the groups were beginning to help each other. I watched as a boy in a wheelchair raced down the path with a boy that could walk. They were laughing as they raced. I hoped the lessons they learned here, would stay with them forever.

The next few days were very busy. There was still a lot to do. Everyone was comfortable with their schedules so even meal times moved quickly with very few problems.

Chapter 7

Activities Day

We played ball, swam and walked. It was great to see so many of the kids opening up and talking. They were gaining more confidence every day. It can be hard to tell the truth about what's happening in your life, but once you do you feel much better. Once you share your secret it gets easier to talk about. Then you can begin working on a solution.

The staff surprised everyone by announcing plans for an activities celebration, on the third Saturday of camp.

Mr. Jones announced, "We are planning relay races, a ping-pong tournament, swimming competitions, sack races, Frisbee and a huge cook out. It took a lot of planning for us to prepare for a celebration this big. We've chosen the teams and purchased the sacks and ribbons. The chef has planned the menu and ordered the food. We'll have ribbons for the winners and lots of fun for everyone. I know the children in wheelchairs can't get into sacks but they certainly can have wheelchair and relay races. They can also play ping-pong and Frisbee. It will be great fun for everyone."

Everyone clapped when Mr. Jones finished talking. A celebration was exactly what everyone needed. Then we'd only have a week left to complete our camp projects and finalize plans for the kids to return home.

I saw Jimmy on his way to the dining room.

He told me, "Jake I'm so excited about all the fun things we're going to be doing in the next couple of weeks. I'm going to sign up for as much as I can. I've never tried out for anything before coming to camp, but now I'm having fun every day. I hate to think about leaving but it really has been a great experience. I feel better about myself then I ever thought I could. Thank you so much for helping me."

I told him, "You're welcome; I've enjoyed it just as much as you have. You're not the only one that hates to think about leaving, everyone is dreading that day. We all have wonderful memories to take back with us, and your counselor will continue working with you after you go home. You've also made some wonderful new friends you might stay in touch with."

Jimmy said, "Thanks again." He smiled and walked into the dining room.

We were all planning for the big day but that didn't interfere with our normal daily activities. There were trips to the beach, crafts, and wonderful nights around the campfire with lots of toasted marshmallows. I was spending every moment I could with the kids. I was there whenever they wanted to talk, play ball or just sit quietly. The kids seemed to be able to really trust me. Finally, all of the planning was done. The activities celebration would be held on Saturday with a treasure hunt on Sunday.

The mood around camp was pure excitement. Most of the kids knew each other by name and functioned like a big family. They were all helping each other. I'd become close to a lot of the kids. I was sure I'd stay in touch with them after camp ended and we all went home.

The staff was talking about having camp there again next year. They asked me to think about coming back if they did. I didn't have to think about it. I knew I'd be there if they were able to do it again next year. The program had been so successful the staff wanted to offer the experience to other kids around the country that needed it.

While I was on my way to the beach one afternoon, Freddie went whizzing down the path in his wheel chair. I hadn't talked to him since the day his chair got stuck in the dirt.

I yelled, "Hey Freddie, wait up, I want to talk to you for a minute."

Freddie told me, "I don't have much time; I'm in a hurry to meet some of the kids to go swimming. I've never had this much fun in my life. I'm doing things here I never thought I could. Well, I have to go"

He yelled bye, as he headed off to the beach to join the others.

Brenda ran up to me and said, "I've been looking for you to tell you what's happened since the night I talked to you about my problem. Susan called my mother and told her everything. She is coming here tomorrow to see me. Mom said my uncle will never hurt me again. The police arrested him and he's going to prison. He'll never come to our house again. Mom said she wished I had told her sooner so she could have protected me. I am so glad she isn't mad at me."

I told Brenda, "Your mother loves you, she wouldn't be mad at you. You didn't do anything wrong, your uncle did. Your mom was worried about you. You're a special girl, in time I hope you'll think so too."

Brenda said, "I hope so too. Susan told me I have the power to stop anyone from ever touching me in a way that I find uncomfortable. She said all I have to do is talk to an adult about what they're trying to do to me, and they'll be stopped."

I told her, "Susan is right. People that hurt children are just as afraid as you are, but they are afraid you'll tell someone and they will be caught and punished, and they should be. You'll never go on being a victim again as long as you can talk to someone."

Brenda thanked me and went to meet some of the other kids. When Brenda left I went down to the beach where some of the kids were playing volleyball. I wished I could hit the ball back over the net like they did. I was better at catch and fetch. After all I was a dog!

I looked out at the water and saw some of the kids practicing for the swimming competition. The teams were just about ready to go. I watched for a while. They were really good. When the kids were in the water they usually just played, so you couldn't tell how well they could swim.

I went back to the main building to see if the other groups were practicing. Sure enough, the ping-pong teams were playing and the Frisbee's were flying outside the dining room. Everywhere I looked the kids were practicing.

Everyone was involved in at least one sport.

I circled around and asked them, "How's it going?"

One of the kids said, "It's going great, we're really having fun."

Saturday should be exciting. Mom and Dad would be coming to help out. I had so much to tell Mom, I was looking forward to seeing them both.

The next couple of days flew by and the big day arrived. Everyone woke up early. The excitement had grown more every day. I went to all the cabins to remind the kids they had to shower, and have breakfast, before the events could start. They were laughing and joking with one another. Most of them had nicknames for each other. Breakfast was the noisiest meal we'd had yet. The kids just couldn't wait to get started. Lunch would be delivered to the picnic area. They wouldn't want to stop the events to go to the dining room on a day like this.

Mom and Dad arrived just in time to join in all the fun. Mom asked me, "Where will they start?"

I told her, "The schedule was planned to allow everyone to watch each event. Since we're in the main building, Ping-pong will be first."

Mr. Jones spoke to the kids before the games began. He told them, "This is to be a day of fun. I want everyone to play fair, share with your camp mates and have a good time. We don't want to have any sore losers here today. You're all winners."

The kids lined up and started to play. All the practicing had really helped.

Freddie said to me, "I didn't think I could play Ping Pong so I never tried, until I came to camp. I feel so good just knowing I can do something like everyone else."

I told Mom, "He doesn't have to allow being in a wheelchair to limit him as much as he had before. He said he was always afraid to try something new, he was afraid he'd fail. If you don't at least try, you'll never know how much you can accomplish."

Frisbee was next and just about everyone competed. There were Frisbees everywhere, and lots of laughs. Some went farther than others, but every one got off the ground.

The kids yelled to me, "Jake, can you get the stray Frisbees for us?"

I ran around and gathered them, then brought them back so they could throw them again. The counselors were busy taking notes. All the ribbons would be given out after the cookout.

The relay racers lined up. The teams would pass a small wooden paddle to each other as quickly as they could, after they took their turn running. There were two categories for the event. The wheelchair racers were on the left, and the other team was on the right.

Freddie started the race for the wheelchair category. He took the paddle, put it into his lap and pushed on his wheels as fast as he could go. He went flying down to where the barrels were set up, went around the barricade and was heading back to the next racer. He passed the paddle on to Lisa, the pretty brunette with the pony tail, and off she went.

I was so happy to watch these kids having so much fun! The kids in wheelchairs gained so much from the competition. So many of them had told me they didn't think they could compete.

It was time for the sack race. Everyone lined up in pairs and got their sacks. All you could hear was laughing everywhere.

Mr. Jones yelled, "Okay get ready!

Then he added, go!"

A long line of kids began at the starting line and raced for the finish. Some of them were laughing so hard, they fell down. It was a most unusual sack race, but everyone had a great time. Somehow there were two winners and everyone cheered.

Swimming was next, then we'd have lunch in the picnic area. There were so many good swimmers it was sure to be a tough competition. There would be three races, the boys against the boys, then the girls against the girls and finally the boys and girls would swim against each other. I wondered how this would turn out.

I heard John telling Linda, with the short curly dark brown hair, "The boys will beat you girls with no trouble at all, we are much better swimmers."

Linda responded by saying, "Don't be so sure of yourself we could surprise you."

I thought she could be right; you just never know.

Mr. Jones blew the whistle and the boys went into the water. They swam very well. I watched closely as two of the boys were tied, finally John won but not by much. Next it was the girls turn, they gave the boys some real competition. It would be interesting to see what happened when they swam against each other.

Mr. Jones blew the whistle and they all jumped in. I watched very closely as the two teams swam. All of a sudden I noticed something was wrong. One of the boys went under the water and didn't come up.

Linda yelled, "Steven needs help."

I ran and jumped in. I swam as fast as I could out to Steven. As I got there his head popped up, and I told him, "Hold onto me and I'll take you back to shore."

Steven was telling me, "No, I can make it myself."

I said, "Not this time, hold onto me and we'll go back to shore. If you're ok you can go back into the water later."

Steven did as I asked. I was so relieved that he was safe. He was a very quiet boy from Montana and this was one of the few times we had spoken.

Everyone came out of the water to check on him. Thankfully he was really fine, he had just gotten a cramp and went under to try and rub his leg.

After a few minutes Mr. Jones told the kids they could complete the last race. The outcome was a real surprise. Nancy, the bubbly red head, and Jimmy ended up in a tie. They both did equally well swimming against each other.

The scores were recorded just in time for lunch. Everyone was starved so they all raced for the food. The chefs had prepared sandwiches, salad, chips and drinks. After lunch, there would be an hour break before starting the next competition. It was a lot cooler, but it was still an

August afternoon and everyone needed time to digest their lunch.

Mr. Jones blew his whistle; it was time to start. The kids were excited; this was what they'd been waiting for. They all lined up, Mr. Jones blew his whistle again, and they were off.

They raced faster than I thought they could possibly go in their chairs. They were all laughing and pushing as fast as their arms could go on the wheels. It was such a joy for me to watch this event. Some of these kids thought they couldn't do anything, before they came to camp. Just look at them now! The race was a perfect end to the day's events. When it was over, everyone was tired.

Mr. Jones announced, "There will be a two-hour break to rest and clean up before the cook-out."

Everyone went back to their cabins. Some of the kids took a nap, and others sat around and talked. It gave me a chance to spend some time with my parents.

Mom told me, "Everything is going well at home. I spoke to Donna and she asked that we say hello to you for her. She has been going out more with her friends."

I told her, "That's great news, I think about her all the time. I'll visit her as soon as I get home.

I told Mom, "I want to come back next year, if they decide to have camp here again. Would you please tell to Mr. Jones I'll come back whenever they need me?"

Mom smiled and said, "I'll be right back, and went to Mr. Jones's office to speak to him."

Chapter 8

The Web Site

Mom caught up with Mr. Jones as he was walking to the main building.

She told him, "Jake would love to come back next year if you need him."

He said, "I'm so glad to hear that. Everyone is extremely pleased with the way Jake has related to the children. He's done a wonderful job. He's really made a big difference for the kids. They have been able to talk to him about anything that was bothering them. In some cases we have made major progress because of his love, patience, and understanding of the children."

Mom told Mr. Jones, "Jake's always been wonderful with children. From the time he was very young it was obvious he was born to do this." She thanked Mr. Jones and came back to us.

The three of us took a long walk around the camp then cleaned up before going to dinner. The Wonderful smells filled the camp as the cooks prepared a side of beef over an open fire. They also prepared lots of wonderful desserts. I'd never forget these meals when I went back home.

After dinner, everyone won a ribbon for one event or another, and then we all went to the campfire area. Mr. Jones spoke to the kids about the days activities then cancelled the stories. Everyone was just too tired from such a busy day. Dad and Mom said good night and left to drive home. They said they'd be back next Sunday to pick me up.

The weeks had gone by so fast; I could hardly believe it was almost time to leave. I was ready for bed too. I'd think about the coming week tomorrow when I woke up.

I had another dream that night. Max talked to me again. He told me, "Jake, you've done a wonderful job with the kids here at camp.

You've handled many different problems. You've always used excellent judgment, and been kind and fair. The Higher Power has not only allowed you to speak to children, He has given you wonderful intuition to know how and when to help them. I don't think you'll need me, but if I can ever help you just think about me and I'll come."

I woke up feeling very pleased about what Max said to me. Then I wondered what all the noise was about; I had forgotten we were having a treasure hunt after breakfast. I was just relaxing like I did at home on a Sunday morning.

Timmy, the freckled red head, ran into the cabin and asked me, "Jake, did you forget about the treasure hunt?"

I jumped up, shook myself off and dashed out the door. I was like a counselor and had to be on time. As I got to the main building everyone was just beginning to arrive for breakfast. That was close. Even though I'd overslept, I'd still made it on time.

Mr. Jones gave everyone instructions for the treasure hunt. He said, "Do not climb to look for clues they are all low enough for everyone to reach. Start in the picnic area to find your first clue."

Some of the kids went in pairs and others in small groups. I tagged along behind to make sure nobody got into trouble, as they set out to find their first clue.

The hunt lasted until lunch. Everyone showed up in the dining room sweating from running and hunting. It was such fun for everyone. It really tested their minds to figure out where all the clues were hidden. The treasures were mostly books. The fun was just finding them.

After lunch we had a free afternoon to do whatever we wanted. The kids could swim, do crafts, lounge in the picnic area or just relax. A free afternoon was just what we needed to recover from the last two days. Everyone was tired from all the activities.

I decided to swim and hang out at the beach for a while. I talked with some of the kids about their plans for after they went home.

Billy, the blonde boy with glasses said, "I want to see if we can organize a group at school to share our experiences. Maybe we could help each other."

I thought that sounded like a wonderful idea. A lot of the kids sounded much more hopeful than when they first came to camp.

David, with the spiked brown hair, spoke up and said, "This has been one of the most enjoyable times in my life. Now I have friends, so I'll never feel alone again."

The next few days went by fast. There was so much to do getting everyone ready to go home. The kids saw their counselor every day and normal camp activities were being held. I stayed close to the kids just in case they needed to talk to me. I would give them my e-mail and post office box addresses before they left. They came to camp and worked very hard, now they were ready to go back home and continue working with their counselors.

They could also get in touch with me whenever they needed to. I asked the kids to give my addresses to any of their friends they thought needed my help. They all said they would.

The kids were all special and they could be anything they wanted to be. They just had to work hard and never stop trying. I told them if anyone ever threatened them or tried to hurt them, they should tell a grown-up right away.

The children all listened and promised they would remember all the things I told them. They told me they'd never forget me, even when they grew up and could no longer hear me speak.

Saturday night there was a very special time around the fire. All of the counselors took turns congratulating the kids for all their hard work, and then Mr. Jones stood up.

He said, "I have a large package of paper and pencils which I'm going to put here on this table. If any of you feel that being at camp has helped you to deal with a bad experience or painful memory, you can write it down on a piece of paper and drop it into the fire. This may help you to leave it behind you when you go home."

Without any conversation one by one each of the kids walked or wheeled over to the table, picked up a piece of paper, and wrote on it.

Then they formed a line and either walked or wheeled over to the fire and dropped their paper in. They were totally silent until the last paper had dropped onto the fire. Then it was as if they were charged with a bolt of energy, they all cheered, "Yeah."

Mr. Jones told everyone, "We are so proud of all of you, and the progress you've made. It's been an incredible experience for everyone. Remember you'll never be alone again. Your counselors, parents, friends and Jake will all be there for you."

The following morning after breakfast, the buses would be taking everyone to the airport, bus station or train station. All of the kids would be traveling with counselors. Everyone was already packed, so it wouldn't take long to get ready in the morning. Of course there would be time for good-byes. I watched the kids as the counselors spoke. They were all quite emotional. What a difference from the group that had arrived just four weeks ago.

The last night of camp most of the kids stayed awake and talked. They could nap on their way home.

Most of the kids seemed to be stalling as they got ready for breakfast. I thought they might have mixed feelings about leaving. They said they were anxious to go home but knew they would miss their new friends. There was a last minute rush to exchange addresses and phone numbers, and there were a lot of hugs and kisses. I gave everyone my addresses. I wished them luck and said good-bye, before I walked back to the main building to meet Mom and Dad. It had been an amazing four weeks. I was so glad I came!

Mom and Dad arrived right on time. Mr. Jones walked out to the car before we left and said, "Jake, I'll call you about next year. Thank you again for the wonderful job you've done." I asked Mom to thank him and tell him I'm looking forward to it, so she did.

Driving out of camp gave us a very different feeling from when we arrived. Four weeks ago we thought the camp was beautiful, now we knew it was powerful too.

The ride home gave me a chance to nap; I hadn't gotten much sleep the night before either. I woke up just as we pulled into the driveway. I looked around; it was really good to be home. Mom said she told my friends I would be tired today and asked them not to visit until tomorrow. I was glad because I needed another nap!

It didn't take long for word to spread around the neighborhood that I was home. All of the kids were anxious to see me. They all said they missed me. Peter, our next door neighbor, asked me, "So, Jake, was it as great as you thought it would be? We want to hear all the details."

I told them, "I missed all of you too. I'd had a wonderful experience at camp. I had the pleasure of meeting a lot of terrific kids from all over the country. I hope I was able to make a difference in some of their lives."

My friends filled me in on what had happened around the neighborhood, and how everyone was doing. It was really nice to be home. When they left, I went in and checked the computer to see if I had any e-mails yet. Mom left it on so I could see it. I thought it was probably too soon to hear from anyone, when suddenly the e-mail symbol popped up.

I got so excited I yelled to Mom, "Mom come quick, I've got mail."

Mom came in and pulled up the message. It started, "Hi, Jake, my friend went to camp with you and I wondered if you could help me with a problem?"

I was so thrilled. Mom smiled then bent down and gave me a hug.

I told her, "Mom it's really working, the kids know all they have to do is write to me, and I'll help them with whatever their problem is."

Let's Talk About It ...

Sometimes it's hard to talk about what's happening in your life, especially when you've been told not to or threatened. If something or someone is hurting you deep inside where no one else can see it, please don't be quiet. Talk to an adult or talk to me, just talk and never stop talking. You have the power to stop anyone from continuing to hurt you. Talk to someone about what's happening. As soon as you tell your secret to one other person you can get help.

Please check out my web site <u>www. onlychildrenhearme.com</u>

You can e-mail me from my web site or at <u>contactjake@onlychildrenhearme.com</u>

Or you can write to me at   Jake
P.O. Box 7327
Warwick, R.I. 02887

If you write to me I will answer you.

Be safe,
Jake

978-0-595-44359-8
0-595-44359-1

Printed in the United States
205213BV00001B/295-372/A